Crawly Bug
and the Firehouse Pie

Weekly Reader Children's Book Club Presents

Crawly Bug
and the Firehouse Pie

By Toby Speed
Illustrated by Margot Apple

NEWFIELD
PUBLICATIONS
Middletown, Connecticut

This book is an original presentation of Newfield Publications, Inc. Newfield Publications offers book clubs for children from preschool through high school. For further information write to: **Newfield Publications, Inc., 4343 Equity Drive, Columbus, Ohio 43228.**

Newfield Publications is a trademark of Newfield Publications, Inc.
Weekly Reader is a federally registered trademark of Weekly Reader Corporation.

Editor: Stephen Fraser   Designer: Veronica McTigue Kelly

ISBN: 0-8374-9802-3

Printed in the United States of America.

For three who can make a pie disappear
Vanessa, Kate, and Zoe
T.S.

For Crawly Bug's father

M.A.

Crawly Bug crept over the sill and stole a crumb
from Mama's hot pie. He carried it back to the nest.

"Yum," said his dozens of brothers and sisters.
They got in line and wriggle-jigged over the daisies,
under the milkweed, over the crab grass, under
the chicory, up the trellis, and over the sill.
One by one they took a crumb.
And the pie disappeared.

"Who took my pie?" cried Mama. "My very last
summertime blackberry pie? My pie for the firehouse sale?"
She sniffed. A whiff of butter was still in the air.
But where? No pie in the oven. No pie in the bread box.
No pie in the china closet. No pie on the windowsill.
No pie anywhere!

Then Mama looked out the window. And who did she see going single file down the trellis, under the chicory, over the crab grass, under the milkweed, over the daisies, and through the yard? Dozens and dozens of bugs wriggle-jigging, each one holding a crumb.

Bop! Mama swiped at them with her mop. But her mop didn't stop them.

Mama ran outside and grabbed the rake.
She raked ridges in the dirt. But Crawly Bug and his
brothers and sisters went up and down, up and down,
over the ridges, holding their crumbs.

Mama planted her big feet in the way.

But Crawly Bug and his brothers and sisters went left and right,

left and right, around Mama's feet, holding their crumbs.

Mama flung her apron on the ground.
But Crawly Bug and his brothers and sisters went
over and under, over and under, through the folds,
holding their crumbs.

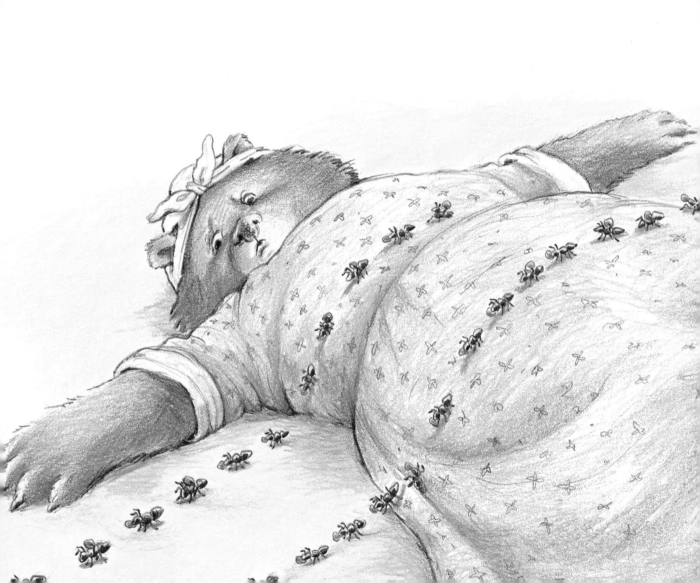

Then Mama lay down in the path. As big as she was, even she couldn't stop Crawly Bug. He and his dozens of brothers and sisters walked right over Mama and kept on going. They went to the end of the yard, and then they went under the fence.

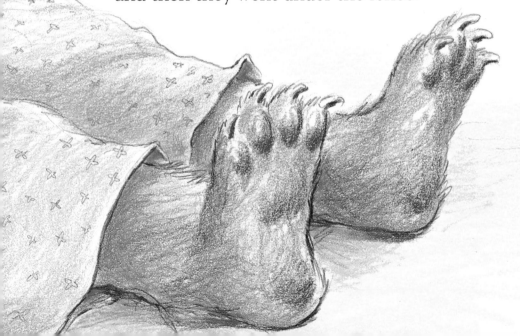

Mama got up and shook herself off. "I promised a
pie for the firehouse sale," she said, "so I'd better bake
a new one quick." Mama looked around the yard. She
looked for a spot of black or a spot of red that might
be a berry.

Is that a raspberry, under a leaf? No, only a bit
of ribbon playing hide and seek.

Is that a cranberry, next to the gate?

No, only a marble that rolled away.

Are those wild strawberries, wedged in a rock?

No, just an old sneaker that went for a walk.

"Now what?" asked Mama. "I can't bake another pie. Every last berry on every last bush went into that blackberry pie."

Then Mama leaned over the fence. Below her, in the tangled vines, the very last bug with the very last crumb was vanishing into a hole. But next to that hole, where she had never looked before, was a fat blackberry bush just covered with fruit! Quickly Mama filled her apron.

"Why, there's enough here for three more pies," said Mama.

And so she baked three.

Two pies she wrapped in hopsacking and huckaback,
and hid in the chimney flue.

The third pie she put in a hatbox, under a Panama hat.
To be safe, she wrote on the the outside of the box NOT PIE.

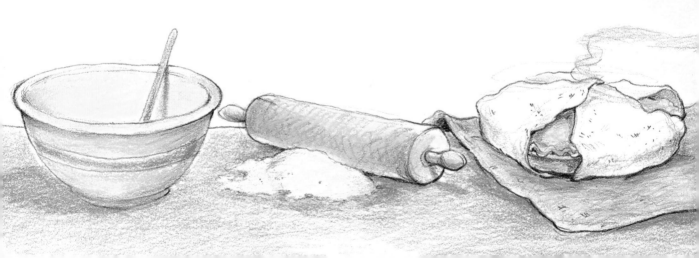

Then Mama tiptoed to the front door.
She looked in and out and up and about,
but she didn't see Crawly Bug or any of his
brothers and sisters.

So she ran with the hatbox to the end
of the lane and up the hill to the firehouse.

The other ladies were already there, setting up their cakes. Mama looked over her shoulder and under the table, but she didn't see Crawly Bug. So she set her hatbox down.

Little by little Mama lifted the cover. She picked up the Panama hat. A gorgeous whiff of blackberry pie spiraled up to her nose. Mmmmm! Mama smiled. But just then SOMEBODY stepped ever so lightly on her toes. Slowly, very slowly, Mama looked under the table.

And who do you think she saw?

Crawly Bug and dozens and dozens and dozens and dozens of bugs! They came all the way to the firehouse sale for second helpings all around!